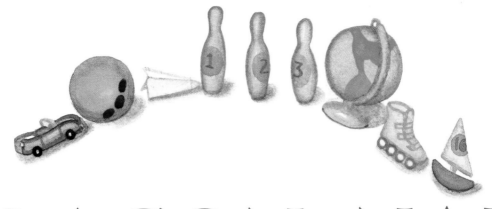

DRAGON NAPS

By Lynne Bertrand   Pictures by Janet Street

VIKING

VIKING
Published by the Penguin Group
Penguin Books USA Inc., 375 Hudson Street, New York, New York 10014, U.S.A.
Penguin Books Ltd, 27 Wrights Lane, London W8 5TZ, England
Penguin Books Australia Ltd, Ringwood, Victoria, Australia
Penguin Books Canada Ltd, 10 Alcorn Avenue, Toronto, Ontario, Canada M4V 3B2
Penguin Books (N.Z.) Ltd, 182–190 Wairau Road, Auckland 10, New Zealand

Penguin Books Ltd, Registered Offices: Harmondsworth, Middlesex, England

First published in 1996 by Viking, a division of Penguin Books USA Inc.

1   3   5   7   9   10   8   6   4   2

Text copyright © Lynne Bertrand, 1996
Illustrations copyright © Janet Street, 1996
All rights reserved

CIP Data is available upon request from the Library of Congress.
ISBN 0-670-85403-4

Manufactured in China
Set in Xavier

For Nick and Georgie
—L. B.

For Dad
—J. S.

ONE day, **TWO** dragons' mothers said these **THREE** words: "Time for naps."

As usual the dragons would rather do anything else. They could build a secret **FOUR**-story tree fort in the woods.

They could play another game of dragon bowl to break their **FIVE**-five tie. They would even prefer to scrub the area underneath the sink, using their fingernails.

However they went straight up to bed and lay staring at the ceiling.

The sheets were crisp and cold and uncomfortable in every way, and the sun shone through the windows into their eyes. Their feet felt **SIX** sizes too big for their skin, and they could hear their friends organizing a game of kickball outside their window.

SEVEN minutes had barely passed when the dragons began to taste the sheets for the flavor of laundry soap

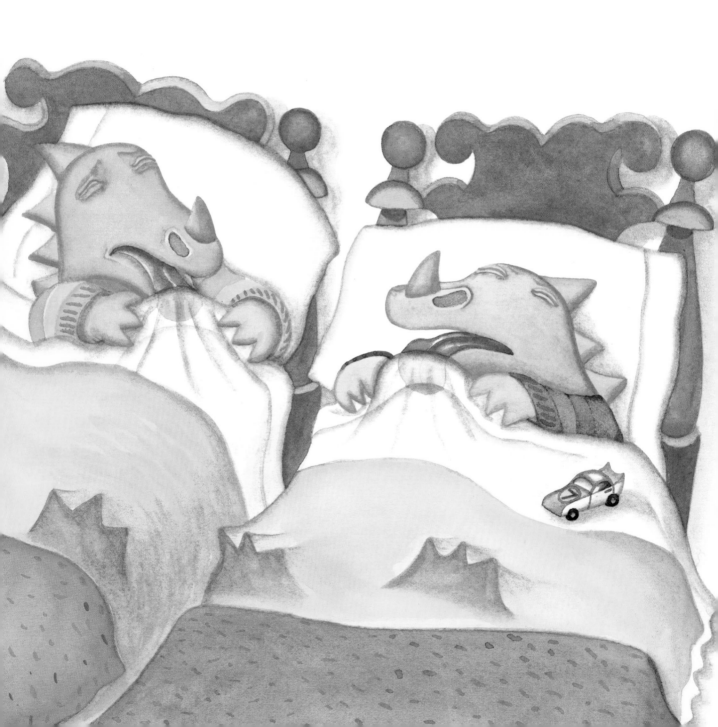

and to notice interesting patterns on the ceiling,
EIGHT feet above.

They put on wax lips and set up the blankets as a
warehouse for pieces of gum they had previously
stored under the bed.

They reached for their pencil sets on the carpet and wrote their names in small, flowery handwriting in **NINE** colors in their diaries.

They counted sounds they could make using only their bodies. After **TEN**, their mothers knocked at the door and said to keep it down to a dull roar. (The only rule about naps, of course, is that you cannot get all the way out of bed. But also it isn't wise to be heard downstairs.)

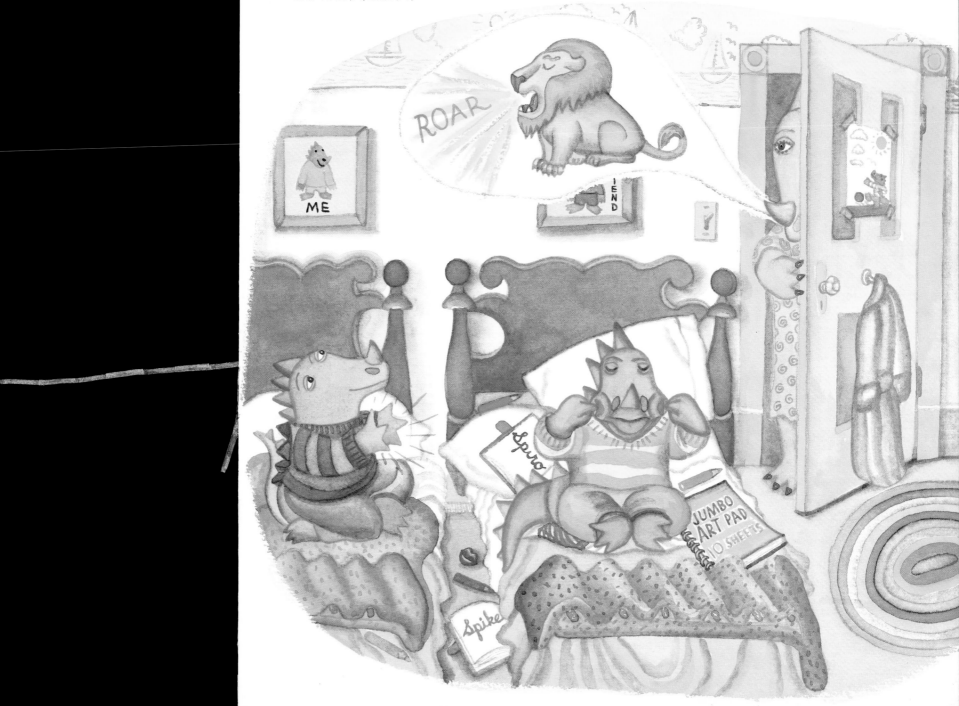

"We can't sleep," they said.
"Count sheep," said their mothers. "Sheep jumping over a fence."

But the dragons became sidetracked on why the sheep were jumping over the fence anyway. They finally decided that **ELEVEN** of the sheep were escaping the farm to play kickball.

The dragons thought of **TWELVE** places where they would like to go for vacation

the Moon

the Ocean

the Biggest
Mountain

12
MILES
TO PEAK

tree fort

camping

the Grand Canyon

grand

and **THIRTEEN** things they would buy, including beds with escape hatches.

They typed up a list of everything they couldn't stand.
(There were **FOURTEEN** items.)

Darkness fell.

The dragons organized a secret code using light switches.
They signalled to each other, using **FIFTEEN** short
flashes, that they couldn't think of anything to say.

They played with the radio and settled on station **SIXTEEN**, which was playing Italian pop tunes about werewolves.

They exchanged compliments.

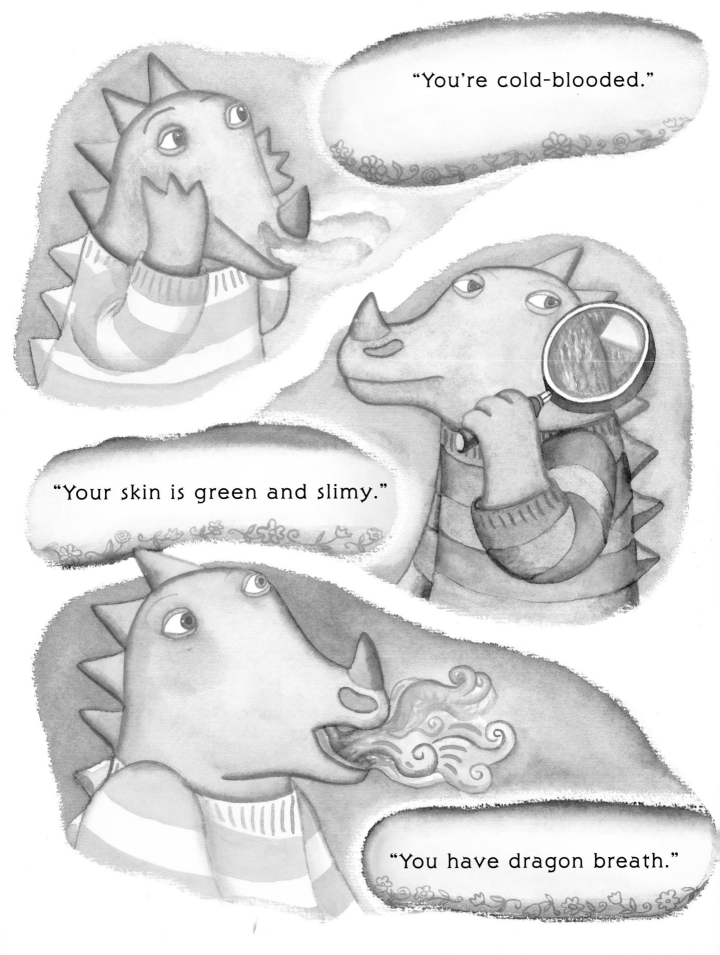

They counted every noise they could hear. Altogether there were **SEVENTEEN**, including a large anchovy pizza being delivered next door and a burst of cheers from the kickball game outside.

The dragons felt they had been in bed for **EIGHTEEN** hours, but of course it wasn't nearly that long.

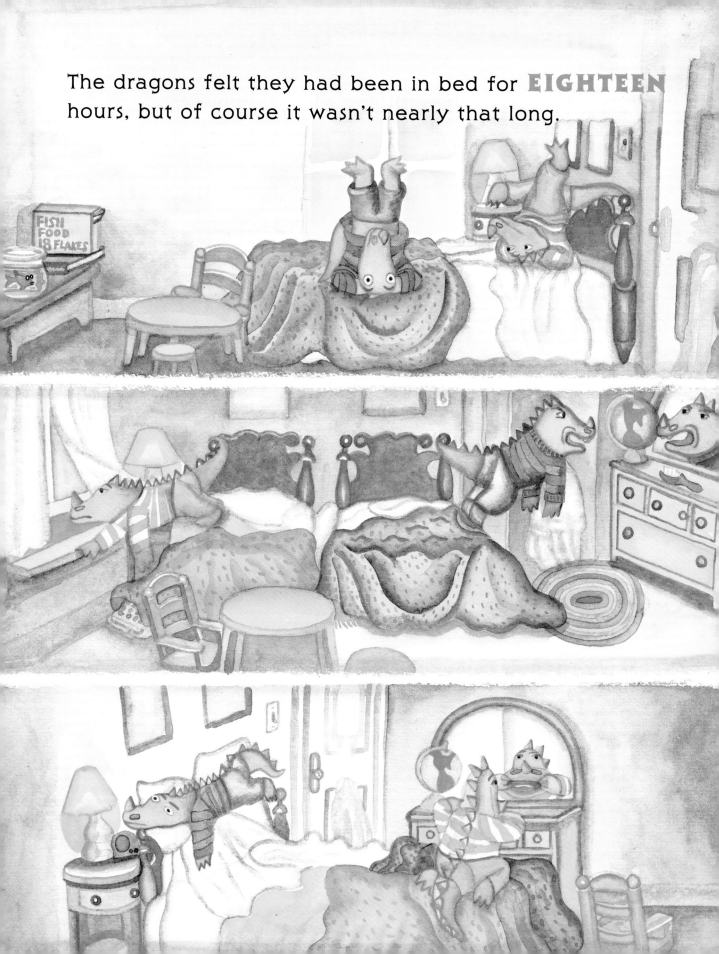

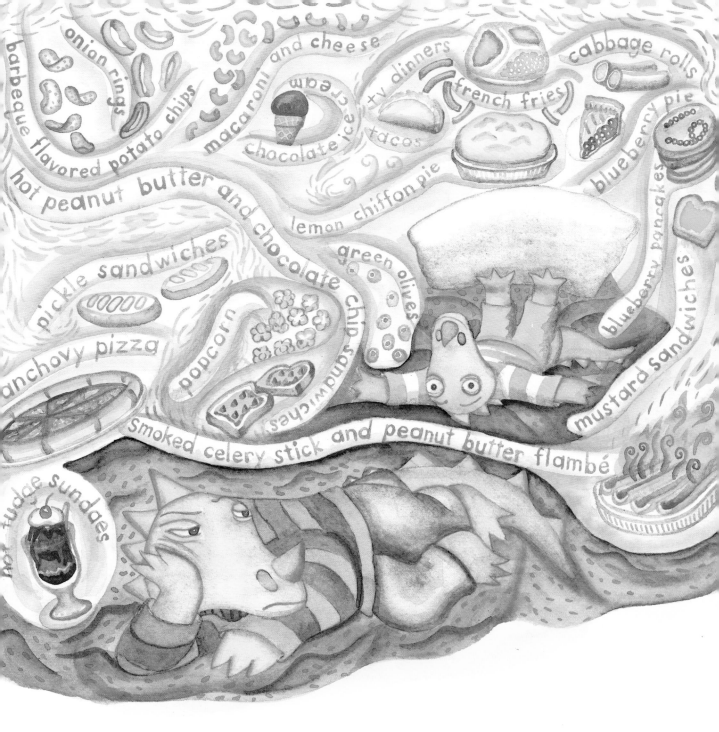

Little did they know that their mothers were about to call them downstairs for smoked celery-stick-and-peanut-butter flambé, which was their **NINETEENTH** favorite food in the world (next to several other fine delicacies).

However, the dragons had just then tried their last resort,

which was to count backwards from a million as fast as they could.

And of course they fell perfectly fast asleep, just when they got to **TWENTY**.